Matthew Kerr

The Ulster Revival of the Seventeenth Century

SALZWASSER
VERLAG

Matthew Kerr

The Ulster Revival of the Seventeenth Century

Reprint of the original, first published in 1859.

1st Edition 2022 | ISBN: 978-3-37513-114-2

Verlag (Publisher): Salzwasser Verlag GmbH, Zeilweg 44, 60439 Frankfurt, Deutschland
Vertretungsberechtigt (Authorized to represent): E. Roepke, Zeilweg 44, 60439 Frankfurt, Deutschland
Druck (Print): Books on Demand GmbH, In de Tarpen 42, 22848 Norderstedt, Deutschland

THE ULSTER REVIVAL

OF

THE SEVENTEENTH CENTURY.

THE ULSTER REVIVAL

OF THE

SEVENTEENTH CENTURY;

AN

INSTRUCTIVE CHAPTER IN THE EARLY HISTORY

OF

PRESBYTERIANISM IN IRELAND.

BY THE

REV. MATTHEW KERR,

DROMORE WEST.

BELFAST:

C. AITCHISON, 9, HIGH STREET.

1859.

TO

THE LORD'S REMEMBRANCERS

IN OUR ZION,

WHOSE EARNEST PRAYERS

FOR A TIME OF REFRESHING GO UP TO GOD,

This Record

OF

THE LORD'S REVIVING WORK

IS DEDICATED.

PREFACE.

IT may be necessary to state how I came to think of publishing this narrative. Having recently to deliver a lecture on "The Ulster Revival of the 17th Century," the necessary preparation brought the subject fully before me. The more I read of the Revival, the greater the interest that gathered around it. Then it struck me that a short account of this remarkable work of grace might stir up some to desire such another season of revival. It is to *Reid's History of the Presbyterian Church in Ireland* I am mainly indebted for the materials out of which this, the most instructive chapter in the history of our Zion, has been compiled. That work is too large and expensive to be generally read—to the many it is altogether inaccessible. In the hope of bringing the subject of the Revival before the minds of some who have not access to the History, and with the desire of stimulating the people of God throughout our Church, these pages have been written.

M. K.

THE MANSE, DROMORE WEST,
April, 1859.

THE REVIVAL IN ULSTER.

CHAPTER I.

WHAT A REVIVAL OF RELIGION IS.

" He shall come down, like showers
Upon the fruitful earth,
And love, joy, hope, like flowers,
Spring in his path to birth."

WHAT is a revival? It is midsummer, and no rain has fallen for weeks. The bottled clouds refuse to yield one drop of moisture, and all nature is sore athirst. Down in the meadows the springs are dried up, and the grass is brown and shrivelled. Here and there the corn fields are red as they were in April, for the green blade has been burned up. Along the wayside the hedgerows are covered with a dense coat of dust. The leaves are drooping, the flowers are dying, the little birds have ceased their song. And as the husbandman surveys his parched fields, and looks up to the brazen sky, his heart sinks within him. But, in His own good time, God hears the cry of universal nature, and sends down the rain. For hours it has fallen copiously, and now the clouds have cleared away, and the sun is shining again. What a change! And how suddenly! All nature is revived. Once more the birds are singing. No longer leaves or flowers are drooping, unless under the load of the rain drops. The fields and hedgerows are green again, for "God has visited the earth and watered it; He has greatly enriched it with the river of God which is full of water."

This is a picture of a revival in the Church of God. When rain from heaven is withheld, the fields of Zion languish; but when the Spirit descends as "rain upon the mown grass and as showers that water the earth," even "The wilderness and the solitary place are made glad, and the desert rejoices and blossoms as the rose." Then, "In the wilderness waters break out, and streams in the desert; and the parched ground becomes a pool, and the thirsty land springs of water." Then sinners are converted and saints are quickened. The Bible is prayerfully read in the closet, and statedly read in the family. The sanctuary is thronged with eager worshippers, and a mighty power accompanies the preaching of the Word; for earnest prayer goes up to God, and ministers preach with the "Holy Ghost sent down from heaven." Then the Church realises the beautiful imagery of the Song of Songs, "The winter is past, the rain is over and gone; the flowers appear on the earth; the time of the singing of birds is come, and the voice of the turtle is heard in our land; the fig tree putteth forth her green figs, and the vines with the tender grapes give a good smell."

But why occupy time in defining what a revival is? Has not the wondrous work going on in America made the subject familiar to every one? Who has not heard of the remarkable spirit of prayer that has been poured out upon all the evangelical churches in the Western World? Whose heart has not leaped for joy at the report of those crowded meetings for prayer in New York and Philadelphia, at midday, attended by business men, willing to give up the busiest hour of the day for a season of communion with God? All have heard of the marvels which the Lord's right arm hath wrought among our American brethren—of the goings of His glorious chariot in its triumphal marches over that great land.   None needs to be told what a revival of religion is.

CHAPTER II.

THE PREPARATORY WORK.

"I will make waste mountains and hills, and dry up all
their herbs; and I will make the rivers islands, and I will
dry up the pools. And I will bring the blind by a way
that they knew not; I will lead them in paths that they
have not known. I will make darkness light before them,
and crooked things straight. These things will I do unto
them and not forsake them."—ISAIAH xlii. 15, 16.

THE Apostle has said that there are " diversities
of gifts, but the same Spirit; and differences of
administrations, but the same Lord; and diversities of operations, but the same God which worketh
all in all." This appears in the different revivals
with which the Church has, from time to time,
been visited. The preparatory work is different
in all. So, too, are the agencies employed.
But the work in every case, so far as it is genu-
ine, is wrought by that " one and the selfsame
Spirit, who divideth to every man severally as
He will." The Ulster revival has features pecu-
liar to itself, as well in its preparatory work as
in its full development. That we may see how

God prepared the way for this work, it will be necessary to glance at the state of things ante-cedent to the revival, as connected, not with Ireland alone, but also with Scotland and England.

Look, first, at *Ireland.* The Reformation was a failure in Ireland. Various causes contri-buted to this. There had been no previous circulation of the Scriptures as in the sister countries; so that when Archbishop Brown was sent over by Henry VIII. to establish the re-formed doctrines in the kingdom, he found the people wholly unprepared to receive them. The Romish faith was abolished by Acts of Parlia-ment, but no efforts were made to instruct the people in the truth. English clergymen, against whom the people were strongly preju-diced, were put into the parish churches. The Irish tongue was then almost universally spoken by the people, and ought to have been employed in the service of the sanctuary. Instead of this, only the English language was permitted to be used, except when the minister could not read English, in which case he was enjoined to use the Latin tongue. No attempt was made to render the Bible or the Service Book into the vernacular of the people. Sir Henry Sydney, the Governor, writing to Queen Elizabeth, in 1576, gives this sad picture of the religious condition of the country : " Your Majesty may believe it, that upon the face of the earth, where Christ is professed, there is not a Church in so miserable a case : the misery of which consisteth in these three particulars—the ruin of the very temples themselves ; the want of good ministers to serve in them when · they shall be re-edified ; and competent livings for the ministers when well chosen." Twenty years later, Spenser, the poet, gives even a more melancholy description of the state of religion throughout the entire country. But of all the four provinces, the condition of Ulster seems to have been the saddest. For years together, divine service had not been performed in any parish church, except in some city or principal town.

The close of Elizabeth's reign in Ireland was disturbed by frequent rebellions. Ulster was the chief seat of these unhappy commotions. The issue was, that the properties of some of the great chiefs were confiscated. These the queen made an effort to colonize with settlers from England, but the project was not successful. When James ascended the throne of England he resolved to colonize Ulster on a large scale, from Scotland as well as England. The way seemed open, as the estates of the revolted Earls of Tyrone and Tyrconnel at this time reverting to the crown, the king had placed at his disposal not less than half-a-million acres of land in the northern province. To Sir Arthur Chichester the direction of the scheme was entrusted, and much of the success of the *Ulster Plantation* is to be attributed to his skilful management. About 1610 the colonists had begun to occupy the confiscated lands. Scotland, from its vicinity to Ulster, and from the hardiness and enterprise of its people, furnished by far the largest share of the settlers. Fixing themselves in the north-eastern parts of the province, the Scotch gradually spread themselves into the interior, while the English for the most part occupied the southern and western portions. There was no strife or discord among the strangers. And now what sudden change takes place over the face of the northern counties ! Ruined cities are rebuilt and re-inhabited. Towns and villages spring up where there were none before. The tall woods fall before the axe of the industrious settler, and cleared fields wave with corn, or are clothed with flocks. The hovels of the natives disappear, and lordly castle, or fortified bawn, or snug farm-house, rises where they stood. Everywhere the fruits that follow in the wake of industry are visible. Not more striking is the transformation going on in any of our colonies now, than that which took place in Down and Antrim, in Derry and Tyrone, when our hardy and thrifty forefathers took up their dwelling there in the reign of James.

What was the religious character of the colonists? Perhaps not worse than the character of our countrymen who are now colonizing the seaboard of Australia, or the mighty forests of Upper Canada. The men who go as the pioneers of civilization to any land, are men of strong nerve and enterprising minds, fitted thus for the work they have to accomplish; but too often setting little price upon the means of grace, as they show by the course they pursue in leaving the vine and fig-tree of their fathers, allured too often by golden visions, for a dwelling beyond the reach of Gospel ordinances. There are, however, noble exceptions, for it is not the thirst of gold or the greed of gain that takes all our colonists away from the mother country. Many exceptions there were among the Ulster settlers. The picture drawn by Stewart, the son of one of the ministers who came over, is evidently a little over coloured. "From Scotland came many, and from England not a few, yet all of them generally the scum of both nations, who, from debt or breaking, or fleeing from justice, or seeking shelter, came hither hoping to be without fear of man's justice, in a land where there was nothing, or but little as yet, of the fear of God. . . . Most of the people were all void of godliness, who seemed rather to flee from God in the enterprise than to follow their own mercy." Blair's sketch is dark enough, but is somewhat relieved. "Although among those whom Divine Providence did send to Ireland, there were several persons eminent for birth, education, and parts, yet the most part were such as either poverty, scandalous lives, or, at the best, adventurous seeking of better accommodation had forced thither, so that the security and thriving of religion was little seen to by those adventurers."

Thus the way was prepared in Ireland for the work of grace soon to begin in Ulster. In all these rebellions and confiscations—in this extensive and successful colonization — we can trace the hand of God.

Glance now at *England.* The Reformation, begun under Henry, carried on during the life of his promising son, arrested in its progress while the bloody Mary sat upon the throne, was firmly established as soon as Elizabeth began her reign. It was not, however, a thorough reformation—it did not pluck up by the roots all the Popish errors. Many of the measures of the English Reformers, in the hope of conciliating the Romanists, were only half measures—a compromise that then, as ever, failed to satisfy. This is very powerfully put by Macaulay in the opening part of his history of England. From the very first there were two parties in the Reformed Church of England: the one zealous for forms and ceremonies; the other, of whom Hooper is the earliest representative, opposed

B

to all forms and ceremonies not wholly sanc-
tioned by the Word of God, and anxious for a
reformation more thorough and complete. The
dissatisfied and reforming party soon came to be
called Puritans. Sadly were they persecuted
throughout the long reign of Elizabeth. Many
of the most godly ministers in England were
driven from their pulpits, because they would
not conform to what they deemed unscriptural
rites. But, as had often happened before in
like cases, the more they were oppressed and
persecuted, the more they grew.

Elizabeth died on the 24th of March, 1603,
and in the month following, James was on his
way to London to take possession of the crown
of England. As he journeyed south, the Puritan ministers met him on the way to state their
grievances, naturally expecting sympathy from
him on account of his Scottish birth and train-
ing. They assured him "That they, to the
number of more than a thousand ministers,
groaned under the burden of human rites and
ceremonies, and cast themselves at his majesty's
feet for relief." Alas! they sought relief in
vain from James. Their hopes were utterly ex-

tinguished in the following year, when the king refused to hear their complaints in the *Hampton Court Conference*, and dismissed them with the ominous words, " I will make them conform, or I will harrie them out of the land." This was no vain threat. And now, while the Ulster Plantation is going on, let us see what is taking place among James's Puritan subjects in England.

Unable to bear the yoke any longer, a goodly number of the suffering Puritans from the eastern shores of England take ship and cross over to Holland, bearing with them a learned and godly minister, named John Robinson. They settle, first at Amsterdam, but soon remove to Leyden ; and at last, after a sojourn of twelve years in the latter place, the exiles resolve to seek a home in the New World. A large body of them strike sail from Delph haven, on the 22nd July, 1620. What befel them afterwards — how the party was divided, and some went back from the enterprise—need not be told. A band of about one hundred, after much tossing, reached New England in the May Flower on the 11th November, 1620—a day

ever memorable ! Who could have foreseen the
issue of that expedition ? These Pilgrim
Fathers were the founders of a great empire.
In the fresh earth of the New World they
planted those great principles of civil and religious freedom which had found as yet an unge-
nial soil in their own land. Long since the hand
of God has been acknowledged in all this. Nor
less is it seen in what was taking place at the
same time in Ulster. There, while New England was affording a refuge to the Pilgrim
Fathers, not a few of the persecuted Puritans
sought and obtained a resting place. This
again was God's way of preparing for the revival
that was to follow.

But turn now to *Scotland.* King James in
the early part of his reign in Scotland, in the
meeting of the General Assembly, had publicly
praised God that he " was born in such a time,
as in the time of the light of the Gospel, and in
such a place as to be king in such a Kirk, the
sincerest Kirk in the world." He had charged
the assembled ministers, doctors, elders, nobles,
gentlemen, and barons, to stand to their purity ;
" and I, forsooth," he concluded, " so long as I

brook my life and my crown, shall maintain the same against all deadly." Not long after, the king was labouring with all his might to rob this sincerest Kirk in the world of all her liberty and privilege. Some disguise was worn in Scotland, but this was entirely cast away as soon as he set foot in England. Then the Church which he had solemnly pledged himself in open Assembly to defend, he sought openly to destroy. The more prominent ministers who would not yield to his wishes, were banished or imprisoned. One of these was the celebrated John Welch, of Ayr. After a banishment of fourteen years, he was permitted, after much solicitation, to return to London, his health having suffered so much that nothing but a return to his native country would, his physicians assured him, save his life. His wife, a daughter of John Knox, obtained an interview with the king, and requested that her dying husband might be allowed to breathe once more the air of his native Scotland. His majesty, with coarse oaths, refused her request, unless she would undertake to persuade her husband to submit to the bishops. " Please your majesty," the noble daughter of a noble sire replied, lifting up her apron as if to receive her husband's falling head, "Please your majesty, I would rather kep his head there." While persecution was raging in Scotland, the Ulster Plantation was making rapid progress. Persecuted ministers fled to Ulster, where, for a time, they were permitted to enjoy security, and preach the Word without fear. Here again the hand of God is manifest. The settlement of persecuted ministers from Scotland in Ulster, is another part of His preparatory work for bringing about the revival of religion in the province.

Such was the work of preparation for the revival. God can make the wrath of man—even the persecution of kings — to praise Him. Rulers, in the carrying out of their own schemes of lust or ambition, are all the while preparing the way for the coming of the Lord.

CHAPTER III.

" I will give you pastors according to mine heart, which shall feed you with knowledge and understanding."— JEREMIAH iii. 15.

" The Holy Ghost said, Separate me Barnabas and Saul, for the work whereunto I have called them."—ACTS xiii. 2.

WHEN God has a work to do, the fitting men are always raised up. All the important eras in the history of the Church furnish illustration of this truth. And never was it more strikingly confirmed than in the Ulster revival. He who, in the early ages of the Church, " gave some apostles, and some prophets, and some evangelists, and some pastors and teachers, for the perfecting of the saints, for the work of the ministry, for the edifying of the body of Christ," sent at this time to Ulster a band of men eminently endowed, and of singular devotedness— men in every way fitted for the work given them to achieve.

It may at first sight seem strange that persecution did not follow the exiled ministers to Ireland. But it is to be borne in mind that little was then known of Ireland at the seat of government. And as the historian has observed, "Provided they were removed out of England and Scotland, where they so frequently opposed his arbitrary measures, James cared little for their existence and influence in this remote and turbulent country."

Of the ministers who came over, some were from England, but more from Scotland. The date of the arrival of the first was 1613, so that the settlers were for some years without faithful Gospel ministrations, as in 1610 the plantation had made considerable progress. They were a little band whom God honoured to begin the revival—only seven in number; but when the work began, that little band was strengthened by the addition of nearly an equal number of faithful and laborious men, who entered with much zeal into the movement, and aided by their counsel, their preaching, and their prayers, to bring about the results that followed. It could hardly be said that the one sowed and the other reaped; for as in those northern regions where the frost and snow have scarce passed away till the song of the reaper is heard as he gathers home the corn, so in Down and Antrim now, the harvest followed fast upon the seedtime, and without enquiring who had sowed, all toiled in the same field, he that sowed and he that reaped rejoicing together. Of the first seven, five were from Scotland and two from England, while of the others who joined them, all were from Scotland, excepting only one. It is not possible in a limited space to give a sketch of each, all we can do is to single out two or three as representatives of the rest.

Of the Englishmen take John Ridge. He had been admitted to deacon's orders by the Bishop of Oxford in 1611, but having no freedom for the exercise of his ministry in England without conformity, he came over to Ireland, and was admitted to the vicarage of Antrim on the 7th of July, 1619, on the presentation of Lord Chichester. Here he laboured with such wisdom and earnestness as to secure from a contemporary the character of "the judicious and gracious minister of Antrim." Another speaks of him as "a great urger of charitable works, and a very humble man." Hubbard and Colwert, his countrymen, were no less gracious or faithful.

Of the Scotchmen take Robert Blair and John Livingstone. Blair had been a professor or regent in the college of Glasgow, but being opposed to Dr. Cameron, the principal, who had been appointed with the view of bringing the college to approve of Prelacy, he threw up his chair, and on the invitation of Lord Clandeboy came over to Ireland in 1623. His own account of his settlement at Bangor, in County Down—the way in which his objections to the place were overcome—his ordination by Mr. Cunningham of Holywood, and the adjacent brethren, the bishop only taking part as a presbyter, to meet his scruples against Episcopal ordination—is exceedingly interesting. His ministry was greatly blessed. One who knew him intimately, thus speaks of him, "He was a man of notable constitution both of body and mind, of a majestic, awful, yet affable and amiable countenance and carriage, thoroughly learned, of strong parts, deep invention, solid judgment, and of a most public spirit for God. His gift of preaching was such, that seldom could any observe withdrawing of assistance in public, which in others is frequent. He seldom ever wanted assurance of his salvation. He spent many days and nights in prayer alone and with others, and was vouchsafed great intimacy with God."

The revival had made considerable way when, in 1630, Livingstone settled at Killinchy, in County Down, and threw himself, with all his heart and soul, into the good work. He had been assistant to the minister of Torphichen, in Scotland, but was silenced by Spotiswood, Archbishop of St. Andrews, because of his opposition to Prelacy. It was under his preaching that the remarkable awakening at the Kirk of Shotts occurred on the Monday after the communion, 21st June, 1630. At this time Livingstone was only twenty-seven years of age, and was acting as chaplain to the Countess of Wigton. Many ministers and people had collected for the communion season. On the Sabbath there was much solemnity, and when the Monday came, all felt reluctant to go away without a day of thanksgiving to Him whose dying love they had been commemorating. Livingstone was prevailed on to preach much against his will, from the deep sense he had of his own unworthiness. Indeed, he had even withdrawn from the congregation to avoid the necessity of preaching, but was moved by a strong impulse upon his mind to return. The result is well known. "I can speak," says Fleming, "on sure ground, that nearly 500 had at that time a discernible change wrought on them, of whom most proved lively Christians afterwards. It was the sowing of a seed through Clydesdale, so that many of the most eminent Christians of that country could date either their conversion, or some remarkable confirmation of their case from that day." Livingstone came to Ireland on the invitation of Lord Clandeboy. Like Blair, he objected to Episcopal ordination, and as in his case, so now—he was set apart by the laying on of the hands of his brethren, the bishop only assisting. Coming from a work of revival in Scotland, his spirit quickened by what he had witnessed at the Kirk of Shotts, Livingstone was, in an especial manner, qualified to assist Ridge and Blair, Welsh and Dunbar, in the great movement God was then carrying on through their instrumentality. His arrival was most opportune.

Thus the men whom God called from England and Scotland to begin or carry on His revival work in Ulster were eminently fitted for the task. Trained all of them in the school of affliction— exiles like John in Patmos, "for the word of God, and the testimony of Jesus Christ"—eminent, not a few of them, for gifts as well as graces, it is manifest to all that they had been separated of the Holy Ghost for the work whereunto they were called.

The position these ministers occupied was a singular one. They preached in the parish churches, and received the parish tithes; and yet they did not give up, the English their Puritanism, or the Scotch their Presbyterianism. There was no compromise on their part. True, this state of things did not long continue. But when the bishops sought to enforce conformity, they were as ready to give up all emolument and submit to trial and banishment for the truth's sake in Ireland, as they had been in Scotland and England. But this comes not before us here. Brave men! Their names are a rich inheritance. Being dead they yet speak to us!

CHAPTER IV.

THE WORK ITSELF.

"And I will make them and the places round about my hill a blessing; and I will cause the shower to come down in his season; there shall be showers of blessing."— EZEKIEL xxxiv. 26.

GOD often works by weak instruments, that the glory may be all His own. Of the ministers who had settled in Ulster, James Glendinning was the least gifted, yet God made use of him to begin the revival. Mr. Hubbard did not survive long his removal to Carrickfergus with his London congregation, and on his death Glendinning was chosen to succeed him. His want of fitness for the place soon became evident to his brother ministers. Blair having occasion to visit Carrickfergus on some business, and hearing him preach occasionally, " perceived," to quote from Stewart, " some sparkles of good inclination in him, yet found him not solid, but weak, and not fitted for a public place and among the English." Blair advised him to remove to some place in the country; and when next we hear of him he is fixed at Oldstone, near the town of Antrim. "He was a man," Stewart tells us, "who would never have been chosen by a wise assembly of ministers, nor sent to begin a reformation in this land. .... Yet this was the Lord's choice to begin with him the admirable work of God, which I mention on purpose that all men may see how the glory is only the Lord's, in making a holy nation in this profane land, and that it was not by might, nor by power, nor by man's wisdom, but by my Spirit, saith the Lord."

At Oldstone Glendinning preached the terrors of the law and God's hatred to sin, and so alarmed a careless people that many were led to cry, "What must we do to be saved?" Rich and poor were awakened. The work spread rapidly. All along the Six-Mile Water valley the cry of anxious sinners was heard. Crowds flocked to Oldstone to hear the Word; still the minister preached only law terrors. He who had raised the storm was not able to allay it; the preacher at whose bidding the waves of spiritual anxiety began to roll, knew not to pour the oil of Gospel grace upon the troubled waters. Like John the Baptist, his message was " Repent," and like him his office seems to have been to prepare men for the kingdom of God, not to lead them into it. Let us not despise the man or his work. The ploughshare deals rather rudely with the fallow ground, but do we reject it on this account ? The hewer in the marble quarry inflicts heavy blows upon the rough unshapen block, but this treatment is necessary to prepare it for the chisel even of a Phidias. At the same time let us see how, in the gifts of the other ministers, God more than supplied what was wanting in Glendinning.

The neighbouring ministers were soon made aware of the work that was going on. Indeed, the excitement had spread to their parishes. They at once came to the help of Glendinning, and by skilfully directing the wounded to the great Physician, many found peace. Soon hope and joy took the place of fear and torment. Meetings for prayer were multiplied, they who were walking in the light desiring to have fellowship one with another. In this way, the *Monthly Meetings at Antrim* originated, that place becoming the centre of the movement. Ridge, the minister of Antrim, "per-ceiving," says Blair, "many people on both sides of the Six-Mile Water awakened out of their security, made an overture that a monthly meeting might be set up at Antrim, which was within a mile of Oldstone, and lay centrical for the awakened persons to resort to, and he in-vited Mr. Cunningham of Holywood, Mr. Hamilton of Killyleagh, and myself to take part in that work, who were all glad of the mo-tion, and heartily embraced it." This was about the year 1626. It was not the common people only who were at this time brought under the power of the truth. "It pleased the Lord," Stewart records, "to visit mercifully the honourable family in Antrim, so as Sir John Clotworthy, and my lady, his mother, and his own precious lady, did shine in an eminent manner in receiving the Gospel, and offering themselves to the Lord, whose example instantly other gentlemen followed, such as Captain Norton and others, of whom the Gospel made a clear and cleanly conquest."

The account of the origin of the Monthly Meetings, as given by Stewart, is the following:

—" When, therefore, the multitude of wounded consciences were healed, they began to draw into holy communion and meeting together privately for edification, a thing which, in a lifeless generation, is both neglected and reproved. But the new life forced it among the people, who desired to know what God was doing with the souls of their neighbours, who, they perceived, were wrought on in spirit as they had been. There was a man in the parish of Oldstone, called Hugh Campbell, who had fled from Scotland; him God caught in Ireland, and made him an exemplary Christian until this day. He was a gentleman of the house of Duket Hall. After this man was healed of the wound given to his soul by the Almighty, he became very refreshful to others who had less learning and judgment than himself. He therefore invited some of his honest neighbours, who fought the same fight of faith, to meet him at his house on the last Friday of the month, when and where, beginning with a few, they spent their time in prayer, mutual edification, and conference on what they found within them. Nothing like the superficial, superfluous meetings of some cold-hearted professors, who afterwards made this work a snare to many. But these new beginners were more filled with heart exercise than head no- tions, and with fervent prayer rather than conceity gifts to fill the head. As these truly increased, so did this meeting for private edification in- crease too ; and still at Hugh Campbell's house on the last Friday of the month. At last they grew so numerous, that the ministers who had begotten them again to Christ, thought fit that some of them should be still with them to pre- vent what hurt might follow."

While Antrim was the centre of the work, it was not confined to it, but extended into the adjoining parishes, spreading over a considerable portion of the north-east of Ulster. The con- gregation of Larne, under the faithful ministry of George Dunbar, shared largely in the awaken- ing. In Bangor, also, as Blair has himself recorded, "The knowledge of God increasing among that people, and the ordinance of prayer being precious in their eyes, the work of the Lord did prosper in the place." At Killinchy, Livingstone was for a time discouraged, for, as he tells us, "although the people were very tractable, yet they were generally very ignorant, and I saw no appearance of doing any good among them; yet it pleased the Lord that in a short time some of them began to understand somewhat of their condition."

'The work of God went on for years without any abatement of interest. Monthly, there was the meeting of all who could attend at the rallying point, Antrim. We give at length the record of these meetings as furnished by Livingstone:—"We used ordinarily to meet the first Friday of every month, at Antrim, where was a great and good congregation; and that day was spent in fasting and prayer, and public preaching. Commonly two preached every fore-noon, and two in the afternoon. We used to come together the Thursday's night before, and stayed the Friday's night after, and con-sulted about such things as concerned the carrying on of the Work of God; and these meetings among ourselves were sometimes as profitable as either Presbyteries or Synods. Such as laid religion to heart, used to convene to these meetings, especially out of the Six-mile-Water valley, which was nearest hand, and where was the greatest number of religious people: and frequently the Sabbath after the Friday's meeting, the communion was celebrated in one or other of our parishes. Among all the ministers, there was never any jar or jealousy; yea, nor amongst the professors, the greatest part of them being Scots, and some good number of very gracious English; all whose contention was to prefer others to themselves. And although the gifts of the ministers were much different, yet it was not observed that the people followed any to the undervaluing of others. Many of these religious professors had been both ignorant and profane, and for debt and want, and worse causes, had left Scotland. Yet the Lord was pleased by His Word to work such a change, that I do not think there were more lively and experienced Christians anywhere than were at this time in Ireland. They were in good numbers, and several of these persons in good outward condition in the world. Being but lately brought in, the lively edge was not yet gone off them, and the perpetual fear that the bishops would put away their ministers, made them with great hunger wait on the ordinances. I have known them come several miles from their own houses to communions, to the Saturday's sermon, and spending the whole Saturday's night in several companies, sometimes a minister being with them, and sometimes themselves alone, in conference and prayer. They have then waited on the public ordinances the whole Sabbath, and spent the Sabbath night in the same way, and yet at the Monday's sermon were not troubled with sleepiness; and so they have not slept till they went home. In those days it was no great difficulty for a minister to preach or pray in public or private, such was the hunger of the hearers, and it was hard to judge whether there was more of the Lord's presence in the public or private meetings."

Blair's testimony is to the same effect—" The blessed work of conversion, which was of several years' continuance, spread beyond the bounds of Antrim and Down, to the skirts of neighbouring counties; and the resort of people to the Monthly Meetings, and communion occasions, and the appetite of the people were become so great, that we were sometimes constrained in sympathy to them, to venture beyond any preparation we had made for the occasion. And indeed, preaching and praying were so pleasant in those days, and hearers so eager and greedy, that no day was long enough, nor any room large enough, to answer their strong desires and large expectations."

The work attracted considerable notice. Fleming, an independent witness, in his *Fulfilling of Scripture*, more than confirms the testimony of Blair and Livingstone. " I shall here instance," he writes, "that great and solemn work of God which was in the Church of Ireland some years before the fall of prelacy, about the year 1628, and some years thereafter, which, as many grave and solid Christians yet alive can witness, who were there present, was a bright and hot sun-blink of the Gospel ; yea, may with sobriety be said to have been one of the largest manifestations of the Spirit, and of the most solemn times of the downpouring thereof, that almost since the days of the apostles hath been seen. I remember, amongst other passages, what a worthy Christian told me, how sometimes in hearing the word such a power and evidence of the Lord's presence was with it, that he hath been forced to rise and look through the church, and see what the people were doing, thinking from what he felt on his own spirit, it was a wonder how any could go away without some change upon them. And then it was sweet and easy for Christians to come thirty or forty miles to the solemn communions which they had, and there continue from the time they came until they returned, without wearying or making use of sleep; yea, but little either meat or drink, and, as some of them professed, did not feel the need thereof, but went away most fresh and vigorous, their souls so filled with the sense of God."

Such was the revival granted to our fathers when God brought them to this land. It was a great work, not confined to one parish, but bringing under its influence a goodly portion of Ulster. It was no evanescent movement, producing a temporary excitement, and then dying away, leaving no traces behind. It extended over a series of years, and its fruits were soon visible.

" O God, what time thou didst go forth,
　　Before thy people's face :
And when through the great wilderness,
　　Thy glorious marching was.

　　.　　.　　.　　.　　.　　.　　.

O God, thou to thine heritage
　　Didst send a plenteous rain,
Whereby thou, when it weary was,
　　Didst it refresh again."

CHAPTER V.

THE ISSUES AND LESSONS OF THE WORK.

"And generations yet unborn,
  Shall praise and magnify the Lord."
                          —PSALM cii. 18.

THE Ulster Revival rooted the truth in the
northern province—rooted it securely. A storm
was gathering that was to try it sorely. When
the tempest swept in fury around it, safely it
weathered the storm. Had the time of trial
come before, instead of after, the revival—had
the bishops enforced conformity at first, or had
the terrible massacre happened twenty years
sooner, very different would have been the
results. It is a living, not a lifeless church that
will stand the fires of persecution. It is only
men who have felt the power of the truth who
will suffer for the truth's sake. When the
massacre was over, the condition of the church
in Ulster was gloomy enough. But, as the wide-
spread cedar, that seems almost crushed to the
earth when the snow storm has fallen, shakes off
its load, and with a bound assumes its former

position, when the first breath of spring has blown upon it; so that church stood up more vigorous than before, when once the gloomy night of popish fury had passed by.

The fruits of the revival are still seen in Ulster. That province is the coldest and bleakest in Ireland. Yet how immeasurably superior it is in every thing to Connaught, or Munster, or even Leinster! We are not insensible to the shortcomings of the descendants of the good men whom God so blessed and honoured, now more than two centuries ago. We are not forgetful of departure from the faith on the part of many; nor of the coldness and deadness of multitudes whose creed is orthodox, and whose forms of worship are scriptural. There is much in the past to mourn over, much in the present we would fain have otherwise. But, when we look at the superior tillage of Ulster, its thriving towns and villages, its busy seats of manufacture; when we think of the loyalty of the large masses of its population, the industry of its middle and lower classes, and the integrity of its merchants and men of business, we cannot help ascribing much of that which has given this province such a proud pre-eminence, to the labours of Blair and Livingstone, and their brethren, and to the remarkable blessing that attended their efforts. We are now reaping what they sowed—sowed often in tears. As yet the results of their work have told mainly upon Ulster. But we are firmly persuaded they are yet to extend a mighty influence on the whole land, over all its length and breadth.

The record of this revival is the most instructive chapter in the history of Presbyterianism in Ireland. Would that we could read the lessons it is fitted to teach! We have a great work to do in Ireland—does it not tell us how we can best accomplish that work—how success is to be attained? In outward organization we were never in so prosperous a condition as now. We are united. No false doctrine is preached in any of our pulpits. Everywhere, in every good work, how much zeal is displayed! At home what doors of usefulness are opening up! In the Colonial field, and in the Foreign and Jewish Mission fields, there are far more calls for help than we are able to respond to. When had we such reason to look with hopeful eye into the future? Never! And if our organization is prosperous, the scripturality of our system too, was at no former period more firmly believed in by our people. Not only are we assured of its derivation from the Word of God, but we are experiencing more and more every day, how admirably fitted it is to advance the kingdom of God in any land, or among any people. In all this we rejoice; for have we not reason to rejoice?

Yet here a danger threatens. We may be tempted to trust in the completeness of our organization, and the scripturality of our system. We may forget that in the building of the Lord's spiritual house, church polity is but the scaffolding, and is only useful as it enables the builders to raise the walls of the glorious structure—that it is only the casket for preserving the priceless jewel of divine truth in the world. And our forms of worship are only the censer in which the incense of the heart—pure spiritual worship —is to be offered to God. We yield to none in our attachment to Presbyterian order and worship, but, God forbid that we should give them a place and an importance they were never designed to hold! Whenever we are tempted to do this, how strong soever we may appear to ourselves or others, God has written Ichabod upon us, and we are truly impotent for good.

If then we would achieve great things, we must be anointed with the oil of heavenly grace —baptized with the Holy Ghost and with fire. Wanting this preparation, we labour in vain, and spend our strength for nought. Hitherto effort has not been rewarded with proportionate success. Why? The presence of the life-giving spirit has been withheld. A bright future is before us. That we may not fail in our high mission in this land, let us seek another revival. If other churches labour more earnestly, manifest more of the Spirit of Christ, seek with greater purity of aim to promote, not their own glory, but the glory of God, they will surely outstrip us in the race; and why should they not? It is true of churches as of individuals— "Them that honour God He will honour." It is a living, earnest, humble church God will bless. And, O with what power we would assail the stronghold of antichrist in our land, if a time of refreshing were granted us from on high !

Are we not encouraged to plead with God for a revival of His work among us ? We can urge His promises, but we can urge too His dealings with our fathers. We can cry, " Wilt thou not revive us *again,* that thy people may rejoice in thee ?"

WHEN GOD WOULD PLANT OUR GOODLY VINE.

When God would plant our goodly vine within this
    land, of yore,
A place where deep its roots might strike He had pre-
    pared before ;
The vine degenerate and wild with fire He did con-
    sume,
That, cast away, our chosen shoot might grow and fill
    its room.
It was a small and tender plant, that had been trampled
    sore
Beneath the feet of cruel men, when carried to our
    shore ;
But, cherished by the Lord of Hosts, and tended by
    His hand,
Its boughs were yet to spread abroad and cover all the
    land !

When God would plant our goodly vine within this
    land, of yore,
A people suffering for the truth He guided to our
    shore :
From Scotland's rugged land they came, a stern and
    stalwart race ;
They came from England's clime, less used danger and
    toil to face.
Where Neagh and Strangford wide expand, by Carrick's
    castled town,—
Where Foyle and Lagan ebb and flow, the pilgrims
    sate them down.
And through long years of struggle sore, as erst their
    fathers prayed,
They joyed that they were free to pray, with none to
    make afraid !

When God would plant our goodly vine within this
    land, of yore,
A band of exiled ministers, brave men, He hither
    bore ;
Dunbar and Stewart, Robert Blair, in sacred lore who
    shone,
James Hamilton of noble blood, and honoured Living-
    stone,

And Brice, and holy Cunningham, and Welsh—from
    Scotland came—
While Henry Colvert, Hubbard, Ridge—did bear an
    English name.
Long ages past these valiant men have gained the
    crown on high,
But though long dead, their work remains—their
    work will never die !

When God would plant our goodly vine within this
    land, of yore,
His Spirit in a mighty flood from Heaven He did
    outpour;
And where the Six-Mile Water flows, o'er many a
    thirsty soul,
As streams in South recalled, He made the swelling
    torrent roll.
And whereso'er the Word was preached in all the
    country wide,
The outpoured Spirit swept along in a resistless tide.
Oh ! 't was a time when opened were windows in
    highest heaven—
A foretaste of the promised time to earth shall yet be
    given !

When- God would plant our goodly vine within this
    land, of yore,
While yet its years were few, he bade the tempest
    round it roar.
Prelatic persecution raged its slender boughs among,
And Popish wrath in massacre swept furiously along.
But like the stately cedar on the brow of Lebanon,
Its roots more firmly clasped the rock, when past the
    storm had gone.
Since then, though ofttimes it hath heard the tem-
    pest's wild uproar,
Unscathed it stands, safe kept by Him who planted it
    of yore !

M. K.